This book belongs to:

_____

_____

_____

First published by Walker Books Ltd.
87 Vauxhall Walk, London SE11 5HJ

Copyright © 2001 by Lucy Cousins
Lucy Cousins font copyright © 2001 by Lucy Cousins

Based on the Audio Visual series "Maisy." A King Rollo Films production for
Universal Pictures International Visual Programming. Original script by Andrew Brenner.
Illustrated in the style of Lucy Cousins by King Rollo Films Ltd.

Maisy™. Maisy is a registered trademark of Walker Books Ltd., London.

First U.S. edition 2001

Library of Congress Catalog Card Number 00-111704

ISBN 978-0-7636-1610-6 (hardcover)—ISBN 978-0-7636-1611-3 (paperback)

12 13 14 15 SWT 20 19 18 17 16 15

Printed in Dongguan, Guangdong, China

This book was typeset in Lucy Cousins.
The illustrations were done in gouache.

Candlewick Press
99 Dover Street
Somerville, Massachusetts 02144

visit us at www.candlewick.com

Maisy's Morning on the Farm

on the Farm

Lucy Cousins

CANDLEWICK PRESS

Maisy wakes up early.

There's plenty of work to do on the farm.

First Maisy feeds
the chickens.
She fills her bucket
with corn.

Here, chickens! Come and have your breakfast.

Next Maisy
feeds the pigs.
They're hungry!

The sheep have lots of tasty grass to eat.

It's time to milk the cow. Moo!

Squish squish,
squirt squirt.

Maisy fills the
bucket with milk.

Now it's time
for breakfast.

Maisy puts cereal
and milk in her bowl.

Little Black Cat
wants milk, too.

Good work, Maisy!
Have a great day!

Lucy Cousins is one of today's most acclaimed author-illustrators of children's books. Her unique titles instantly engage babies, toddlers, and preschoolers with their childlike simplicity and bright colors. And the winsome exploits of characters like Maisy reflect the adventures that young children have every day.

Lucy admits that illustration comes more easily to her than writing, which tends to work around the drawings. "I draw by heart," she says. "I think of what children would like by going back to my own childlike instincts." And what instincts! Lucy Cousins now has more than thirteen million books in print, from cloth and picture books to irresistible pull-the-tab and lift-the-flap books.